Aggie Gets Lost

Lori Ries

Illustrated by Frank W. Dormer

Charlesbridge

To David, Daniel, Katie, Jennifer, Ross, Emily, and my moms and dads, with love—L. R.

For Mary, who finds me when I'm lost—F. W. D.

Text copyright © 2011 by Lori Ries
Illustrations copyright © 2011 by Frank W. Dormer
All rights reserved, including the right of reproduction in whole or in part in any form.
Charlesbridge and colophon are registered trademarks of Charlesbridge Publishing, Inc.

Published by Charlesbridge
85 Main Street
Watertown, MA 02472
(617) 926-0329
www.charlesbridge.com

Library of Congress Cataloging-in-Publication Data
Ries, Lori.
    Aggie gets lost / Lori Ries ; illustrated by Frank Dormer.
        p. cm.
    Summary: Ben and Aggie are playing in the park when she chases a ball and does not return, but after looking for her and worrying about her, Ben speaks with his blind friend, Mr. Thomas, who suggests a different approach.
    ISBN 978-1-57091-633-5 (reinforced for library use)
[1. Lost and found possessions—Fiction. 2. Dogs—Fiction. 3. Blind—Fiction.]
I. Dormer, Frank W., ill. II. Title.
PZ7.R429Agg 2011
[E]—dc22   2010007533

Printed in China
(hc) 10 9 8 7 6 5 4 3 2 1

Illustrations done in pen and ink and watercolor on 140-lb. cold-press
    Winsor and Newton paper
Display type set in Tabitha and text type set in Janson
Color separations by Chroma Graphics, Singapore
Printed and bound February 2011 by Yangjiang Millenium Litho Ltd.
    in Yangjiang, Guangdong, China
Production supervision by Brian G. Walker
Designed by Susan Mallory Sherman

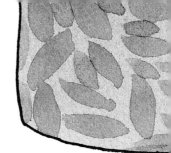

The Bad Day

Left foot, right foot, two feet, four feet.
We walk to the park.
Aggie pulls hard.
She wants to play fetch.

At the park, I unclip Aggie's leash.
I toss the ball.
"Get it, Aggie! Get the ball!" I say.
Aggie is a good dog. She brings it back.

This time I drop it behind me.
Aggie is a smart dog. She finds the ball again.
"Good girl," I say.

"Okay, Aggie. Here is a *hard* ball," I say.
I wind my arm fast. I throw the ball.
It flies up, up, up, and far, far away.
I cannot see my red ball.

"Arf! Ruff! Ruff!" Aggie runs and runs.
Now I cannot see my dog.

I wait and wait.
But she does not come back.

I call her.
"Aggie! Come, Aggie! Here, girl!"

I look for her.

But she does not come back.

I am sad.
I do not see Aggie anywhere.
I walk home slowly.

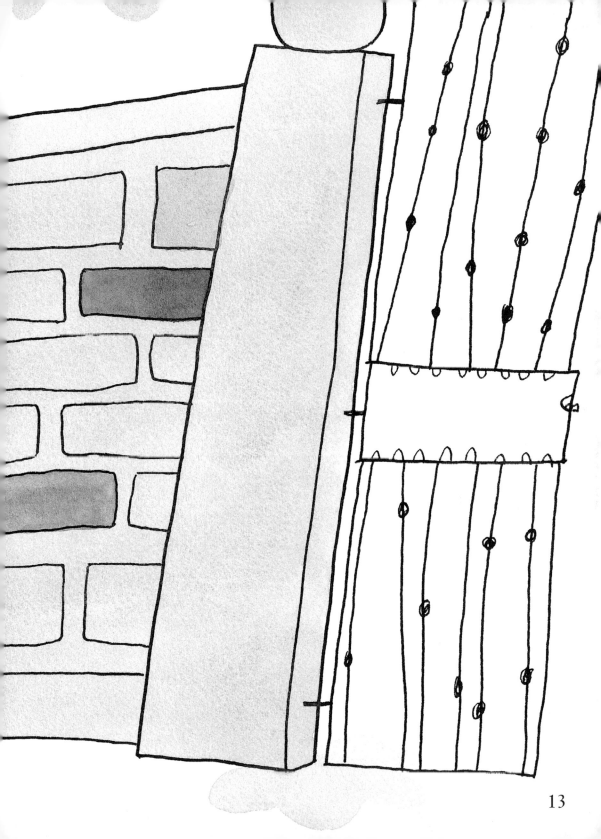

"She was not at the swings," I tell Daddy.
"She was not at the pond," I tell Mommy.
"How can I find Aggie?" I ask.

We make a plan.
Mommy makes phone calls.

Daddy makes pictures.

I make my posters BIG.

Then we go back.
We go back to the park where I lost Aggie.

We tell the kids at the swings about Aggie.

We tell the people at the pond.

We tell the policeman with the shiny badge.

No one has seen Aggie.
It is a bad day.

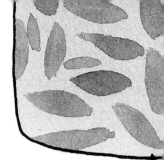

The Awful Night

Aggie is not on my bed.
She is not under my bed.

I look out the window.
"Where are you, Aggie?" I whisper.
I see a wishing star. I wish hard.
"I wish Aggie was not lost!"

I feel sadder.

I think.
What if Aggie is not lost?
What if she ran away?
What if Aggie was not happy?

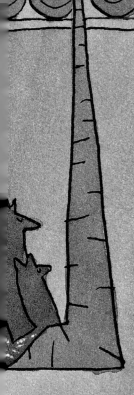
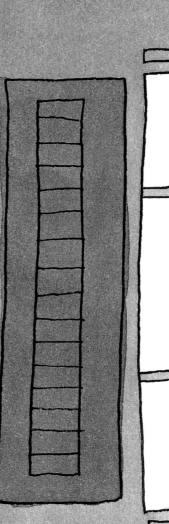

Did I give her enough treats?
Did I pet her enough?
Did I tell Aggie she was a good dog?
I cannot sleep. I am too sad to sleep.
It is an awful night.

I climb on my bed. I look at my toes.

I do not like how Aggie chews things.

I do not like cleaning up her messes.

I do not like her smelly breath.

But I love my dog.
We have fun. We are friends.
We play tug of war.

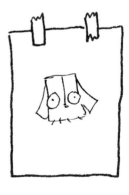

We make snow angels.
We share a room.

I lie on my bed with Aggie's leash.
Aggie was not at the swings.
She was not at the pond.
She is not on my bed.
But Aggie is somewhere.
And I am going to find her.

Found!

The next morning I get up early.
I brush my teeth. I get dressed.
I fill my pockets with treats.
"Let's go back to the park," I say.

Mommy goes one way. Daddy goes another.
We look for Aggie.
She is nowhere.

Mr. Thomas sits on a bench.

"Ah, my two . . . Where's that Aggie?" he asks.

I tell Mr. Thomas about my lost dog.

"I've looked everywhere," I tell him.

"I cannot find Aggie!"

I feel sad again.

"I think she ran away," I say.

35

"Maybe I can help," Mr. Thomas says.

"You cannot help," I say. "You cannot see."

"I can see just fine," Mr. Thomas says.
"Not with my eyes, but there are other
ways to see."

He stands up.
"I use my hands. I use my ears.
I use my nose," he says.
"You've tried using your eyes.
Now try to see like me."

I close my eyes to see like Mr. Thomas.
I feel a cool breeze.
I smell smoky hot dogs.
I hear squirrels chattering, kids laughing,
a bee buzzing, and . . .
something else.
It is quiet and far away.

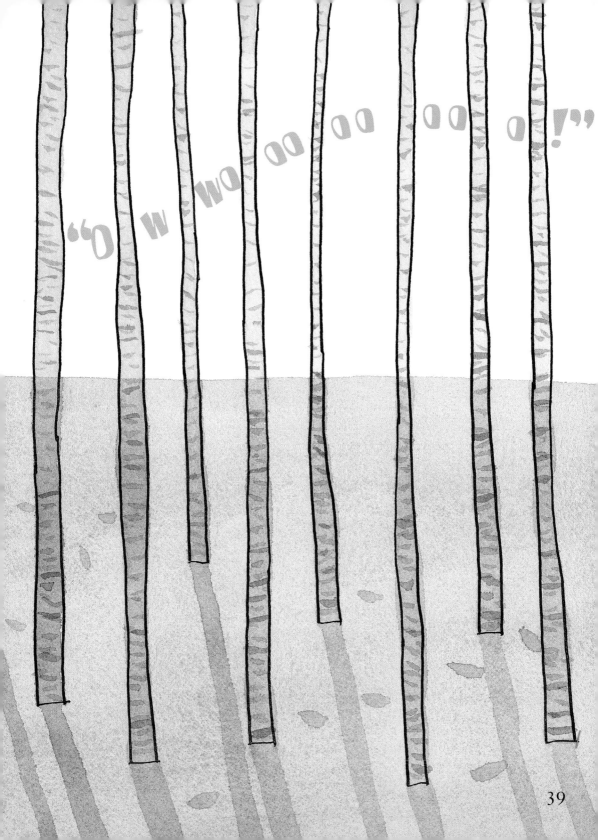

39

"I know that sound, Mr. Thomas!" I say.
I run for the trees.
The howl is closer now.
I run fast!

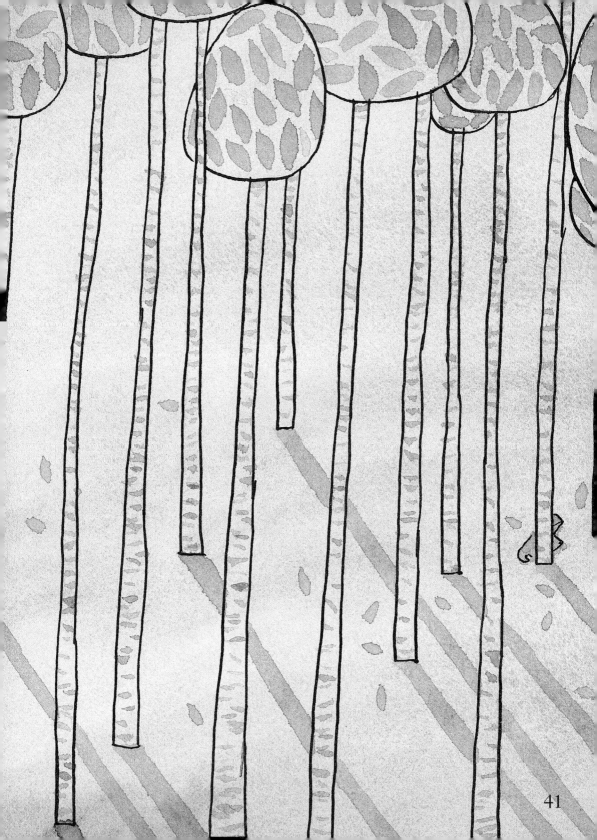

41

"Owwooooo!"

Aggie howls and rolls in the grass.
"Aggie! Oh, Aggie! I found you!" I shout.
I run to Aggie. Aggie runs to me.
She jumps into my arms.
We howl and roll together.

Aggie looks happy.
She feels scratchy.
And she smells—

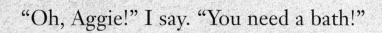

"Oh, Aggie!" I say. "You need a bath!"

Aggie and I are happy.

We walk past the pond.
"I found my dog!" I tell the people.

We walk past the swings.
"I found my dog!" I tell the kids.

We find Mommy and Daddy with
Mr. Thomas and the policeman.
"I found Aggie!" I say.

Mommy and Daddy are so happy,
they almost cry.

Left foot, right foot, two feet, four feet.
We walk home.
Aggie gets a head start.